# FIRST DOG
## Unleashed in the Montana Capitol

Written by
**JESSICA SOLBERG**

Illustrated by
**ROBERT RATH**

FARCOUNTRY
PRESS

HELENA, MONTANA

*Many heartfelt thanks to Governor Brian Schweitzer and his staff,*
*First Lady Nancy Schweitzer,*
*Caroline Patterson and Kathy Springmeyer at Farcountry Press,*
*children's book author Gayle Shirley,*
*educators Deb Johnson and Cindy Yarberry,*
*Deb Mitchell at the Montana Historical Society,*
*and Mrs. Ness and Mrs. Moore's third grade class*
*at Hawthorne School in Helena.*

Softcover:
ISBN 10: 1-56037-419-5
ISBN 13: 978-1-56037-419-0

Hardcover:
ISBN 10: 1-56037-425-X
ISBN 13: 978-1-56037-425-1

Illustrations and book design by Robert Rath

For more information on our books, write Farcountry Press, P.O. Box 5630, Helena, MT 59604;
call (800) 821-3874; or visit www.farcountrypress.com.

Cataloging-in-Publication Data is on file at the Library of Congress

Created, produced, and designed in the United States.
Printed in China.

12  11  10  09  08        3  4  5  6

Page 35 illustration by Lucy Rath

Photo credits:
Photos on pages 38-39 courtesy of the Montana Historical Society Archives: J.K. Toole, no date, photograph by Howard J.
Lowry, Helena; John E. Rickards, no date, photograph by Howard J. Lowry, Helena; Robert B. Smith, circa 1898, photographer
unidentified; Edwin Lee Norris, no date, photographer unidentified; S.V. Stewart, no date, photograph by E.C. Schoettner, Butte;
Joseph M. Dixon, April 15, 1904, photograph by Parker, Washington, D.C.; John E. Erickson, no date, photograph by Zubick;
Frank H. Cooney, no date, photographer unidentified; W. Elmer Holt, no date, photograph by W.H. Tippet, Billings; Roy E. Ayers,
no date, photograph by Titter Studio, Great Falls; Sam C. Ford, no date, photograph by Dewalt Studio, Helena; John W. Bonner,
no date, photograph by Dewalt Studio, Helena; J. Hugo Aronson, 1951, photograph by Titter Studio, Great Falls; Donald G.
Nutter, no date, photograph by Hester Studio, Billings; Tim M. Babcock, no date, photographer unidentified; Forrest H.
Anderson, no date, photographer unidentified; Thomas Judge, no date, photographer unidentified; Ted Schwinden,
no date, photographer unidentified; Stan Stephens, no date, photographer unidentified; Marc Racicot, 1993, photograph by
The Montana Department of Transportation Staff Photographer; Judy Martz, no date, photographer unidentified; Brian Schweitzer,
no date, George Lane.

I don't know how many dogs you've met, but I bet none of them has a story like mine.

My story is about how a little cow dog from a small town in Montana—that's me!—came to work with the governor in the state capitol.

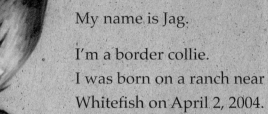

My name is Jag.

I'm a border collie.
I was born on a ranch near
Whitefish on April 2, 2004.
I was the last pup born
in a litter of 8!

All of my brothers and sisters are special in some way.

One is the oldest.     One is fastest.     One is the silliest.     One can herd better than all the rest.

Jag is more special than he thinks. Did you know that he has one brown eye and one blue eye?

One is an expert at tongue twisters: "The cat catchers can't catch caught cats!"

One can howl with perfect pitch...

...and one can catch Frisbees in mid-air.

Me, I'm just "the last pup."

Let me tell you how the last pup grew up to be the First Dog!

When I was just 7 months old, the people of Montana chose a member of my human family to be governor. My brothers and sisters stayed behind, and my human family left our quiet ranch and moved to the capital city, Helena.

They took me with them.

**November 8, 1889:**
Montana becomes
the 41st state.

**1894:**
Helena becomes the capital city.

"Good-bye, little Jag," my brothers and sisters said as we loaded up the pickup truck and bounced down the gravel road.

I live with the governor's family in the governor's mansion.
It's a big house just for governors.

Every morning I get up early and go straight
to my bowl in the kitchen for breakfast.

"Let's go, Jag!" the governor says, when he
finishes his toast and eggs.

Then the governor and I walk two blocks to the capitol.

When dogs live in groups, one dog serves as the leader. This dog is usually bigger and stronger than the rest. When people live in groups, they all get together and pick their leaders. This means anyone can be the leader, not just the biggest or strongest!

In the United States, we live in a democracy. Democracy means "rule by the people."

The governor is chosen by the people of Montana in an election.

Election Day is the first Tuesday in November. On that day, everyone gets together and votes in secret for the person they want to lead the government in the state.

After the governor serves for 4 years, the people get together again and decide if they want to reelect that person (keep him or her as governor) or choose someone else.

**1959:** The governor's mansion was designed and built to look like a ship.

The governor is the top person in charge of government in Montana—kind of like the president of the state.

Government is what runs Montana. We need government to take care of things such as roads and schools.

Who votes in elections? If you will be 18 by the day of an election, you can vote! How many years until you can vote?

| Year you were born: | | Year you can vote: |
|---|---|---|
| 2005 | >> | 2023 |
| 2004 | >> | 2022 |
| 2003 | >> | 2021 |
| 2002 | >> | 2020 |
| 2001 | >> | 2019 |
| 2000 | >> | 2018 |
| 1999 | >> | 2017 |
| 1998 | >> | 2016 |
| 1997 | >> | 2015 |
| 1996 | >> | 2014 |

The dogs here in the city are different.
They aren't cow dogs like me.

"Hi," I say to the first dog I see. "Know any good places to chase cows?"

"Woof," he says, sticking his nose up in the air and walking away. "You must be new around here."

It's no different with the curly-haired dogs. Or the fancy dogs. They all look down their snouts at me. Except the little dogs.

They look up and yip.

The governor and I walk up to a big,
funny-shaped building called the capitol.
This is some fancy barn!

On the lawn, instead of herds
of cows and sheep, there are squirrels
everywhere, racing from tree to tree.

Do you know the
difference between a capital
and a capitol? The capital is the city
where the state's government is located.
The capitol is the building. So, the capitol
is in the capital! Montana's capitol opened
on the Fourth of July 1902. The land
was purchased for just $1!

Atop the capitol stands a mysterious lady. No one knew who she was until 2006.

Her name is *Montana*, and she is a 17-foot-tall statue. She wears a flowing gown and holds a torch in one hand and a shield in the other. A man in Pennsylvania made the statue around 1895.

How many domes do you think the capitol has? If you guessed 2, you're right!

There are actually 2 domes, one inside the other. From outside, you see the large metal dome with small, round windows. From the inside, you can see a beautiful, stained-glass dome. But there is a room in between these 2 domes. And on the ceiling are the signatures of the people who have climbed the winding spiral staircase to see it. Some of the signatures are from the men who built the dome.

Oh, how I want to chase those herds of squirrels!

We climb the steps
of the capitol and
walk down the long
hallway to the
governor's office.
The floor is so shiny
I can see my reflection.

The hall echoes with
the sounds of hurried
footsteps and people
talking on cell phones.
This place is so busy.
It's not quiet like
the ranch.

One of the governor's jobs
is to make sure the laws are
carried out correctly. Laws are
just like rules. You probably
know all about rules at school.

Here are some other things
governors do:
• Come up with ideas about
how to make Montana great.

• Send the state's military
to help out during floods
and fires.

• Communicate with the
governors of other states.

• Greet important guests
visiting the state.

• Dedicate new
buildings.

The governor settles into his big, soft chair and begins to work: writing, talking on the phone, meeting with people.

There are so many people!

I can barely find a place to sit with all the feet and stacks of papers around!

I find a quiet place under the desk to hide.

"Psssssst!"

What's that? I wonder. An office cat?

"Psssssst!  Hey!"

The sound is coming from the window. It is ever so slightly opened.

I stick my nose out and sniff.

"Hiya, Jag," says a squirrel, from the other side of the glass. "Whatsamatter? Cat got your tongue?"

This catches me by surprise. Squirrels are kind of like gophers, and the gophers back home never said a word.

"Oooh, is that a nut?" Sid suddenly bolts, leaving me alone at the window.

"What do squirrels know, anyway?" I say, heading back to my hiding spot.

"I'm Sid," the squirrel says. "Nice to meetcha.
Hey, for a black-and-white pooch, you sure seem blue.
Isn't it fun to be the big dog around here?"

"I'm the *only* dog around here," I tell him.

"Aw, you're just lookin' at it the wrong way," he says.
"I like to sit here and watch 'em run around from room
to room, shufflin' papers, comin' and goin'."

"Watch who?" I ask.

"You know, these two-legged types," Sid explains.
"Big things happen here, but this place isn't just for them.
It's for us little guys, too. That's why we're glad you're here."

Another job that governors have is to sign bills. No, not phone bills. A different kind of bill.

A *bill* is an idea for a new law or a change to an existing law. People come up with the idea for the new law, and then the legislature decides if it's a good one. The governor can sign it (make it a law) or veto it (cancel it).

As I listen to all the excitement above—the phone ringing, people talking—I figure out that the people in the capitol seem to be on two different teams: Democrats and Republicans.

Sometimes they get along, and sometimes they don't.

Dogs aren't Democrats or Republicans.

We're just dogs.

Suddenly, something big and gray smacks into the window.

It sort of looks like one of the chickens back on the ranch.

The bird pokes its little beak into the open window and says, "Hello there, Jag. I'm Phoebe. I'm a pigeon."

Wow, this bird not only talks—but she knows my name!

"We pigeons have been living around the capitol for a long time," says Phoebe, straightening her ruffled feathers. "If you want to know what goes on around here, just ask us."

I tell her that all I really want to know is where the other dogs are.

Phoebe says there aren't any other dogs here. There's just me.

That can't be! I drop my head to my paws.

"Listen, meet me at the window in the House Chamber. Take the secret passage!" she says, pointing to a small opening in one of the walls.

I press against the wall and it moves like a door. I slip through the passage into a room with a fireplace.

Dodging feet, I sneak down the hall until I see the door that reads House Chamber, just as Phoebe said.

There is a secret passage between the governor's office and his reception room! The secret door is found next to the fireplace. It looks just like the wall, except there's a small knob that allows it to open like a door.

Over the fireplace is Governor Toole's picture. Toole was the very first governor of the State of Montana.

Then I see it. Another dog!

I run to the end of a very large room where a dog is walking through some grass.

"Hello!" I say to
the dog, who
stares straight
ahead.

"Incoming!"
yells Phoebe,
who again smacks
into the window.
"Oh, hon, that's
just a painting—
not a real dog."

As I get close,
I see she's
right.

The dog Jag sees in the painting is a wolf. It is standing next to Lewis and Clark in a painting made by Montana's most famous artist, Charles M. Russell.

"This room is where the House of Representatives meets," says Phoebe. "They work together with the governor, senators, and judges to make Montana great. See, it's kind of like the branches on a tree."

"Oh, great," I say. "More people and more piles of paper."

My ears and tail droop. "And no dogs."

There are three "branches" of state government.
1. **Executive Branch:** the governor and executive staff
2. **Legislative Branch:** senators and representatives
3. **Judicial Branch:** judges

**Executive Branch**
The governor is the top person in the Executive Branch. The governor signs bills to make laws and makes sure the laws of the state are carried out correctly.

**Legislative Branch**
The Legislative Branch has 2 groups: 50 senators and 100 representatives. They get together in January every 2 years and meet for 90 days. They come up with ideas for new laws. Anyone can watch the legislature at work. Ask your parents or teacher to take you.

**Judicial Branch**
Judges make up the Judicial Branch. They make decisions about the laws that the legislators create and the governor signs.

Government is not just for "old people!"
Kids of any age can speak to the legislature about bills they believe in. It doesn't matter how old you are, you can voice your opinion and be a part of the process.

25

"Jag!" a familiar voice calls.

My ears perk up.
The governor is calling me.
I say good-bye to Phoebe
and race back to him.

He's got his coat and my leash, and we're out the door. We just got here and we're leaving already. Governors sure move around a lot.

Before I know it, we're at the airport running toward a small airplane with roaring engines. The pilot says the weather is great where we're headed.

I get my very own seat on the plane. I watch out the window as we speed faster and faster down the runway.

Suddenly the plane's nose tips up and we are launched into the sky. Helena grows smaller and smaller below us.

We fly over cities, farms, mountain ranges, and wide, open prairies.

I look out the window and imagine my sister herding cows back in Whitefish. I wonder if my brother is still entertaining the barn cats with his tongue twisters.

They'd never believe the last pup in the litter was flying through the clouds in an airplane.

In SIZE, Montana is the 4th largest state.

In POPULATION, Montana is 44th, with about 940,000 people.

Besides squirrels and
Frisbee, parades are a
cow dog's favorite thing.

Montana is a
BIG state with a
small population.
In a state like
Montana, governors
can meet many of the
people who vote...
but that's still a lot
of hands to shake.
Jag likes to shake
paws, too.

When the plane lands in
Glendive, the governor
and I hop in a pickup truck.

I smile and sniff the breeze
as we drive down the
highway to a parade.

I stick close to the governor as he waves to the crowd and shakes hands. He brought our football, and he throws it to the kids along the parade. The kids laugh and toss it back.

Oh, how I want to chase that ball!

The governor again lobs the football. This time it's to a little girl with two dark braids. Beside her is a tiny pup, staying close by her side to avoid being stepped on.

The governor is the "citizens' advocate," which means governors must get to know the people all around this large state and make sure their voices are heard back at the capitol, where the decisions are made.

"Wow! Are you really the First Dog?" asks the awestruck pup.

"Nah, I'm just a cow dog from Whitefish," I say. "I grew up on a ranch, the last pup in the litter."

The little girl with two dark braids smiles and throws the ball right back to the governor.

"Look at you now!" the little dog says, with an
excitement only puppies have. "You're not the
last pup anymore—you're the First Dog!"

Suddenly, the girl with the dark braids
hugs me tight around my neck.

"Well, if I can be First Dog,"
I tell the pup, "anyone can!"

A few weeks later,
I'm hanging out in the
governor's office, in my
favorite place under his desk.
He's opening letters from kids
around Montana.

He leans down and shows me one
very special letter. It's from
the little girl with the
dark braids.

Inside is a drawing of her behind the governor's desk, with her pup sitting proudly at her feet.

Jag realizes he has a job at the capitol. He helps the governor reach out to the people of Montana and make friends. Without Jag, the little girl might not have known she can one day be governor—and her pup First Dog!

These days, I trot proudly past the fancy dogs out on walks.

Some of the little dogs still yip, and the curly-haired dogs mostly still ignore me.

But it's ok because I'm a dog with an important job.

I help the governor make friends with the people of Montana—in the largest cities and the smallest towns. And I inspire even the littlest kids—and pups—to dream big.

So, every day, I wave at Sid and Phoebe, leap up the steps, and run across the slippery floor in the rotunda.

**1. Joseph K. Toole**
1889 – 1893

**2. John E. Rickards**
1893 – 1897

**3. Robert B. Smith**
1897 – 1901

**4. Joseph K. Toole**
1901 – 1908

**5. Edwin L. Norris**
1908 – 1913

**6. Samuel Stewart**
1913 – 1921

I race down the Hall of Governors, past the one
with the bushy eyebrows, and the one with the
furry beard, and the one with
the handlebar mustache.

**7.** Joseph M. Dixon
1921 – 1925

**8.** John E. Erickson
1925 – 1933

**9.** Frank H. Cooney
1933 – 1935

**10.** William E. Holt
1935 – 1937

**11.** Roy E. Ayers
1937 – 1941

**12.** Samuel C. Ford
1941 – 1949

**13.** John W. Bonner
1949 – 1953

**14.** John Hugo Aronson
1953 – 1961

**15.** Donald G. Nutter
1961 – 1962

**16.** Tim. M. Babcock
1962 – 1969

**17.** Forrest H. Anderson
1969 – 1973

**18.** Thomas L. Judge
1973 – 1981

**19.** Ted Schwinden
1981 – 1989

**20.** Stan Stephens
1989 – 1993

**21.** Marc Racicot
1993 – 2001

**22.** Judy Martz
2001 – 2005

And at the very end of the hall is a picture of my governor. Next to him—sitting proudly—is me, First Dog.

**23. Brian Schweitzer**
2005 –

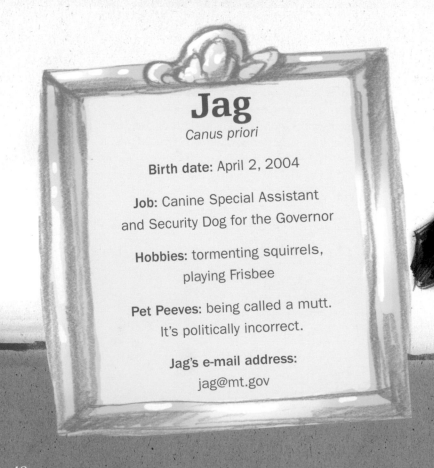

# Jag
*Canus priori*

**Birth date:** April 2, 2004

**Job:** Canine Special Assistant and Security Dog for the Governor

**Hobbies:** tormenting squirrels, playing Frisbee

**Pet Peeves:** being called a mutt. It's politically incorrect.

**Jag's e-mail address:** jag@mt.gov

And that's how the littlest pup went on to do the biggest things!

# GLOSSARY

**bill:** A bill is an idea for a new law or a change to an existing law. People come up with an idea for a new law, and then the legislature decides if it's a good one. The governor can sign it (make it a law) or veto it (cancel it).

**capital:** A capital is the city that is home to the state's government. Every state has one capital city.

**capitol:** A capitol is the building that houses the government in the capital city.

**constitution:** A constitution is a written document that lists the rules and principles regarding how the state is governed.

**democracy:** Democracy is a type of government in which the people rule. The word democracy means "rule by the people." It is from the Greek demos, which means "people," and kratos, which means "rule."

**election:** Elections are how we choose our leaders. As soon as you turn 18, you can register to vote in elections.

**executive branch:** The executive branch is one of three branches of government. The governor and the executive staff make up this branch.

**government:** Government is the system that keeps our communities running. Government takes care of things like schools and roads.

**governor:** The governor is the top person in charge of government in Montana—kind of like the president of the state. The governor is part of the executive branch of government.

**house of representatives:**
The house of representatives is one part of the legislature, or legislative branch.

**judicial branch:** The judicial branch is one of three branches of government and is made up of judges. They make decisions about the laws that the legislators create and the governor signs.

**law:** A law starts out as an idea. The legislature then writes a bill. Then the governor either signs the bill into law, or he or she vetoes it, or cancels it.

**legislative branch:** The legislative branch is one of three branches of government. Representatives and senators make up this branch.

**legislator:** A legislator is someone who serves in the legislature.

**legislature:** The legislature is a group of representatives and senators, who make up the legislative branch. The legislators get together in January of odd-numbered years and meet for 90 days. They meet to solve problems in the state and come up with bills for the governor to sign and make into law.

**representative:** A representative is a member of the house of representatives, which is one part of the legislative branch. There are 100 representatives. The length of their terms is 2 years. They can serve for 8 years before stepping down.

**rotunda:** A rotunda is the round main room in most capitols. Most rotundas have a dome.

**senate:** The senate is one part of the legislature, or legislative branch.

**senator:** A senator is a member of the senate, which is one part of the legislative branch. There are 50 senators. The length of their terms is 4 years. They can serve for 8 years before stepping down.

**term:** A term is the length of time a person serves in office. The term for the governor in Montana is 4 years. Montana governors can serve 2 terms. That means they can serve for 8 years before stepping down.

**veto:** A governor can veto (or refuse to sign into law) an idea for a law (a bill) from the legislature.